HENRY'S IMPORTANT DATE

To librarians, parents, and teachers:

Henry's Important Date is a Parents Magazine READ ALOUD Original — one title in a series of colorfully illustrated and fun-to-read stories that young readers will be sure to come back to time and time again.

Now, in this special school and library edition of *Henry's Important Date,* adults have an even greater opportunity to increase children's responsiveness to reading and learning — and to have fun every step of the way.

When you finish this story, check the special section at the back of the book. There you will find games, projects, things to talk about, and other educational activities designed to make reading enjoyable by giving children and adults a chance to play together, work together, and talk over the story they have just read.

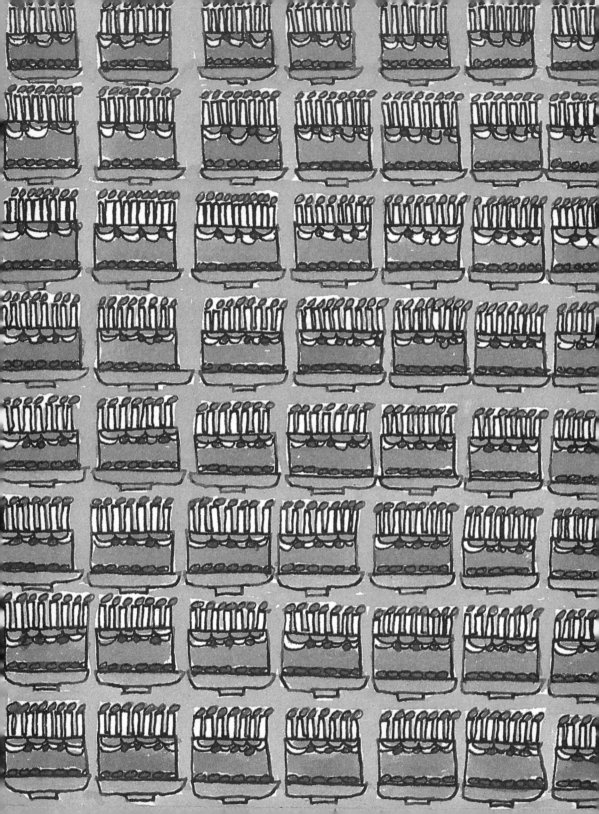

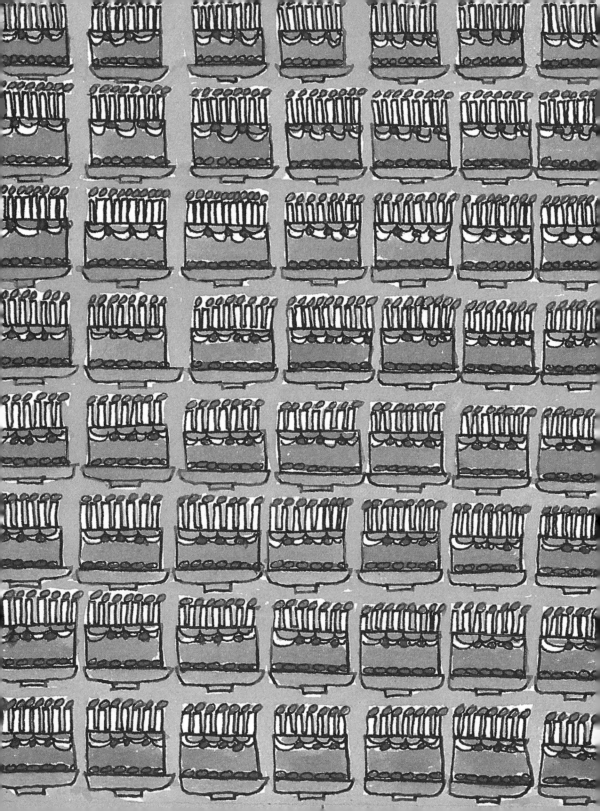

Parents Magazine READ ALOUD Originals:

Golly Gump Swallowed a Fly
The Housekeeper's Dog
Who Put the Pepper in the Pot?
Those Terrible Toy-Breakers
The Ghost in Dobbs Diner
The Biggest Shadow in the Zoo
The Old Man and the Afternoon Cat
Septimus Bean and His Amazing Machine
Sherlock Chick's First Case
A Garden for Miss Mouse
Witches Four
Bread and Honey
Pigs in the House
Milk and Cookies
But No Elephants
No Carrots for Harry!
Snow Lion
Henry's Awful Mistake

The Fox with Cold Feet
Get Well, Clown-Arounds!
Pets I Wouldn't Pick
Sherlock Chick and the Giant
    Egg Mystery
Cats! Cats! Cats!
Henry's Important Date
Elephant Goes to School
Rabbit's New Rug
Sand Cake
Socks for Supper
The Clown-Arounds Go On Vacation
The Little Witch Sisters
The Very Bumpy Bus Ride
Henry Babysits
There's No Place Like Home
Up Goes Mr. Downs

Library of Congress Cataloging-in-Publication Data

Quackenbush, Robert M.
    Henry's important date / by Robert Quackenbush.
        p. cm. — (Parents magazine read aloud original)
    Summary: Due to circumstances beyond his control, Henry arrives at Clara's birthday party just before he thinks it will end.
    ISBN 0-8368-0969-6
    [1. Time—Fiction.] I. Title. II. Series.
[PZ7.Q16Hf 1993]
[E]—dc20   93-7772

This North American library edition published in 1993 by Gareth Stevens Publishing, 1555 North RiverCenter Drive, Suite 201, Milwaukee, Wisconsin 53212, USA, under an arrangement with Parents Magazine Press, New York.

Printed in the United States of America

1 2 3 4 5 6 7 8 9 98 97 96 95 94 93

HENRY'S IMPORTANT DATE

by Robert Quackenbush

GARETH STEVENS PUBLISHING • MILWAUKEE

PARENTS MAGAZINE PRESS · NEW YORK

For Piet
and Margie

A Parents Magazine
Read Aloud Original

On the way to his friend Clara's birthday party, Henry the Duck got caught in traffic.

10

The traffic jam got worse and worse.
Henry did not want to be late
because he had Clara's birthday cake.
But the party was to start
at two o'clock.
And it was already
ten minutes to two.

At five minutes to two,
Henry saw a parking space
and began parking his car.
He thought that if he ran
to a quieter street
he would find a taxi
to take him to the party.

At exactly two o'clock,
Henry's car was parked.
Then he remembered that
the birthday cake was inside.
So were his keys!
He had locked the keys
and the cake inside the car!

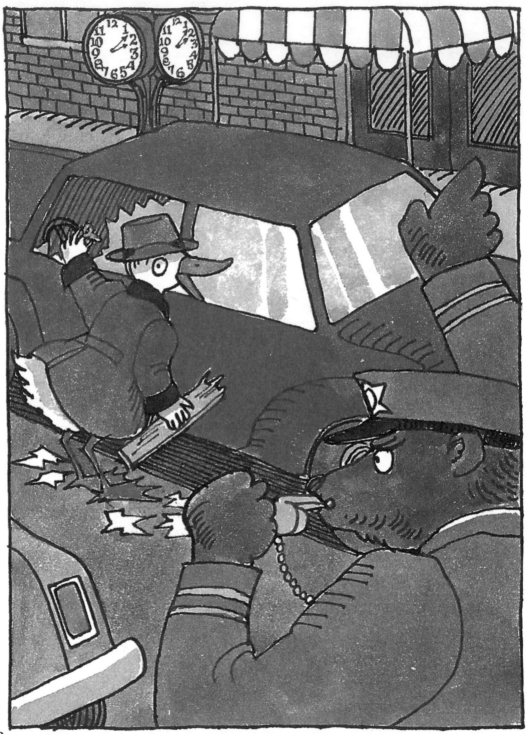

At eight minutes after two,
Henry tried to pry open a window.
The window broke!
"Stop in the name of the law!"
called a police officer.
He thought Henry was a car thief.
So Henry showed the officer his license.
It said, "Henry the Duck."
The policeman let him go.

At twenty minutes after two
Henry ran to get a taxi.
But every one was full.

When a bus came along at two thirty,
Henry decided to take it.
He climbed aboard and
heaved a sigh of relief.
At last, he was on his way
to Clara's party.

But suddenly, at twenty minutes to three,
the motor sputtered and then stopped.
Henry waited and waited
for the bus to go again.

Henry wondered if he would
ever get to Clara's party.
The party would be over
by five o'clock.
And it was already
fifteen minutes to three!

At three o'clock,
the driver opened the bus doors.
"Everybody off!" he said.
"This bus is out of order."
Henry went to call Clara
to say he was on his way.
But he couldn't find a phone.

At twelve minutes after three,
Henry decided that the only way
to get to Clara's was to run.
But as he went tearing
down the street,
he bumped into a shopper
carrying a lot of packages.

Henry helped the shopper
pick up her packages
at twenty minutes past three.
Then he ran on with his own.
The shopper thought Henry
had one of her packages.
"Stop, thief!" she cried.

32

A crowd began chasing Henry
and caught up with him
at twenty-five minutes after three.
A police officer was called.
It was the same one as before.

At three thirty,
Henry opened the package
to show that it was his.
When the shopper saw the cake,
she said she was sorry
about the mistake.
Once again, the policeman
let Henry go.
Henry ran as fast as he could.

At ten minutes to four,
Henry got to Clara's
apartment house.
He jumped on the elevator
and pushed the button
to Clara's floor.
But half way there,
the elevator got stuck.

Henry pushed the bell for help.
A mechanic came to help him
at four o'clock.

At four thirty, Henry
was out of the elevator.
He raced up eight floors
to Clara's apartment
and rang the bell.
Clara opened the door.

"Happy birthday, Clara," said Henry.
"I'm sorry I'm late."
"Late?" asked Clara, surprised.
"But, Henry…

my birthday is not until tomorrow!"

Notes to Grown-ups

Major Themes
Here is a quick guide to the significant themes and concepts at work in *Henry's Important Date:*

- Punctuality: Henry believed it was important to get to the party on time.
- Telling time: every page shows a clock and tells the time on that clock.

Step-by-step Ideas for Reading and Talking
Here are some ideas for further give-and-take between grown-ups and children. The following topics encourage creative discussion of *Henry's Important Date* and invite the kind of open-ended response consistent with many contemporary approaches to reading, including Whole Language:

- If your child is not ready to learn to tell time, this book can help by showing how clock hands keep moving no matter what we do. There's counting involved, too. Don't bother about the minutes (some of which count backward), but count the hours: after two o'clock comes three o'clock, and so on, with twelve being like zero, followed by one.
- For the child who is ready to learn to tell time, this is an amusing way to learn to read time off analog clocks. Although many modern clocks have digital read-outs, reading the time in *Henry's Important Date* will teach children how to use traditional phrases like "ten to three" instead of "two-fifty."

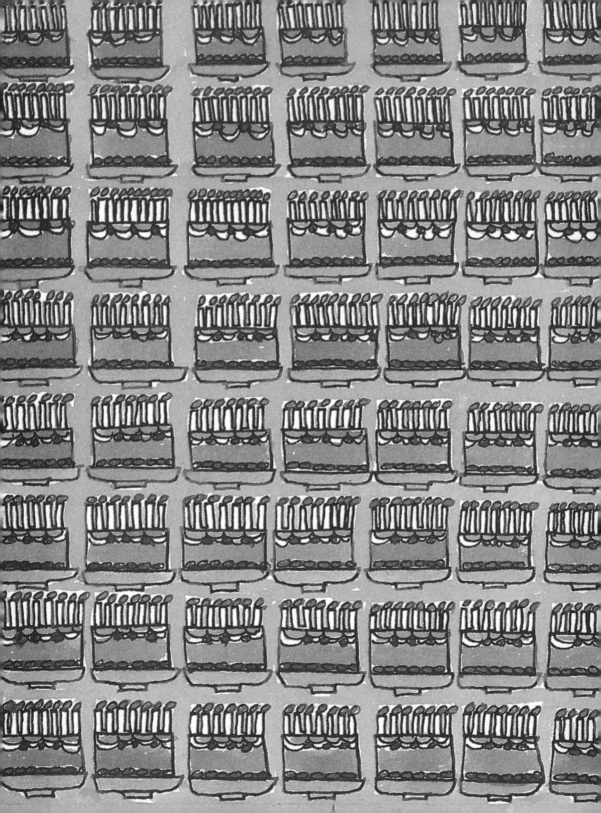

Games for Learning

Games and activities can stimulate young readers and listeners alike to find out more about words, numbers, and ideas. Here are more ideas for turning learning into fun:

Beat the Clock

Learning to tell time is an important skill that involves not only number recognition but also the concept of time itself. To give your child experience in both, teach one special hour at a time (bedtime, dinner, lunch, or time for a favorite television program are good ones to start with). Then help your child set a kitchen timer and see if she or he can "beat the clock" while doing an activity appropriate to the hour (getting into pajamas, putting all the forks around the dinner table, washing and drying hands before lunch, putting away toys before the TV show). Reward success by giving your child a "timely" present: set the timer for extra minutes in which the child may listen to one more page of a bedtime story, play out-of-doors, or watch TV that day.

About the Author/Artist

ROBERT QUACKENBUSH's last name means "duck in the bush" in Dutch. It was originally given to one of his ancestors who was a duck farmer in Holland a long time ago. So it is not surprising that Mr. Quackenbush is the creator of Henry the Duck. The author got the idea for *Henry's Important Date* when his six-year-old son was learning how to tell time.

Mr. Quackenbush is the author/illustrator of more than forty books and the illustrator of another seventy. His artwork has been exhibited in leading museums across the United States. He teaches painting, writing, and illustrating in New York City.

E
Q   Quackenbush, Robert

            Henry's important
            date

Anderson Elementary

 GUMDROP BOOKS - Bethany, Missouri